by ADELAIDE HOLL

Illustrated by

LEONARD WEISGARD

LOTHROP, LEE AND SHEPARD CO., INC., NEW YORK

© 1963 by Lothrop, Lee & Shepard Co., Inc. L.C.C. No.: 63-16778. All rights reserved.
Weekly Reader Book Club Edition. Printed in the U.S.A. by American Book–Stratford Press, Inc., N.Y.

In days of old,
 And times gone by,
When knights were bold
 And castles high,

There lived in the town
 Of East North Devon
A little boy
 Whose name was Kevin —
A smallish lad,
 Not quite eleven.

While the other boys
    Were playing ball
Or trying to scale
    The Old North Wall,

Or sailing little
    Paper boats
Around and around
    In castle moats,

Kevin would sit
    By the king's great door
Watching the knights
    Ride forth to war.

"Some day," said Kevin,
    "I'll be a knight!"
And his eyes were shiny
    As candle light.

The townsfolk smiled
    At what he was saying.
The other boys laughed
    And went on playing.

But in Kevin's heart
    Was a secret dreaming
Of armor and lances
    And banners streaming;

Of galloping off
    With a clink and a rattle
To slay a dragon
    Or fight a battle.

Then, lo! one day
    As he sat outside,
The castle gates
    Swung open wide.

Ta-ta-ta! The royal
    Trumpet carolled,
And forth marched Sir Humbert,
    The king's own herald.

"HEAR YE!" he shouted
    Loud and clear.
Townsfolk came running
    From far and near.

"ood folk of Devon,"
　　Sir Humbert cried,
"A monster stalks
　　Through our countryside!

"It isn't a giant;
　　It isn't a dragon.
But it's high as a house
　　And broad as a wagon.

"It goes with a clash,
　　And a crash, and a rattle.
It smashes our barns.
　　It frightens our cattle.

"Our bravest knights
　　Have fled the land,
And disaster stalks
　　On every hand!"

The townspeople trembled
　　Like leaves in a breeze.
Then they ran into houses.
　　They climbed into trees.

They dived into haystacks
　　And barrels and stables.
They hid under benches
　　And fences and tables.

Did I say *everyone?*
    No, not quite!
There still stood Kevin
    With eyes all bright,

With shoulders high,
    And uplifted head.
"I'll fight this monster!"
    Brave Kevin said.

His small, small voice
    Seemed loud as thunder.
People peeked out of,
    And over, and under.

People said, "Oh!"
    And "Ahhhh!"
        And "Ooooo!"
As out they peered
    For a better view

While straight
    Toward the castle
    Marched little Kevin,
The bravest lad
    In the town of Devon,
A smallish boy,
    Not quite eleven.

is footsteps sounded
    Brave but small
As he pattered along
    Down the marble hall.

And there he stood —
    Quite, quite alone —
Eyeing the king
    On his golden throne.

With a puzzled smile
    The king looked down.
"What's this?
    The bravest man in town?"

He started to laugh
    In sheer surprise.
Then he saw the look
    In Kevin's eyes.

"Brave men," thought the king,
    "Are like gifts and surprises.
They come in all shapes,
    And they come in all sizes."

He sent for his queen,
    He sent for his sages,
His silversmith, armorsmith,
    Swordsmith, and pages.

There was scurrying, hurrying,
    Bustling about. . . .

hen CLANG!
　　went the drawbridge,
　And Kevin swept out!

He was dressed in armor,
　All shiny and bright.
His helmet was plumed
　With red and white.

He carried a sword,
　And a shield, and a mace.
But proudest of all
　Was the look on his face.

He mounted his steed.
　He flourished his sword.
Then he galloped away
　While the townsfolk roared.

He rode into mountains,
   Higher, and higher,
Till he came to a cave
   Near Abbingsfordshire.

And there he found . . .
The monster?
   No!
Just a little old man
   With a beard like snow.

"Good Sire," said Kevin,
   "I have come from the East.
I am seeking a monster,
   A terrible beast!"

"Alas and alack, Sir,"
   The old fellow stated,
"That hideous beast
   Is a thing I created!

"I'm a harmless old man,
   And my name, Sir, is Amos.
I'm a sort of inventor,
   Though not really famous.

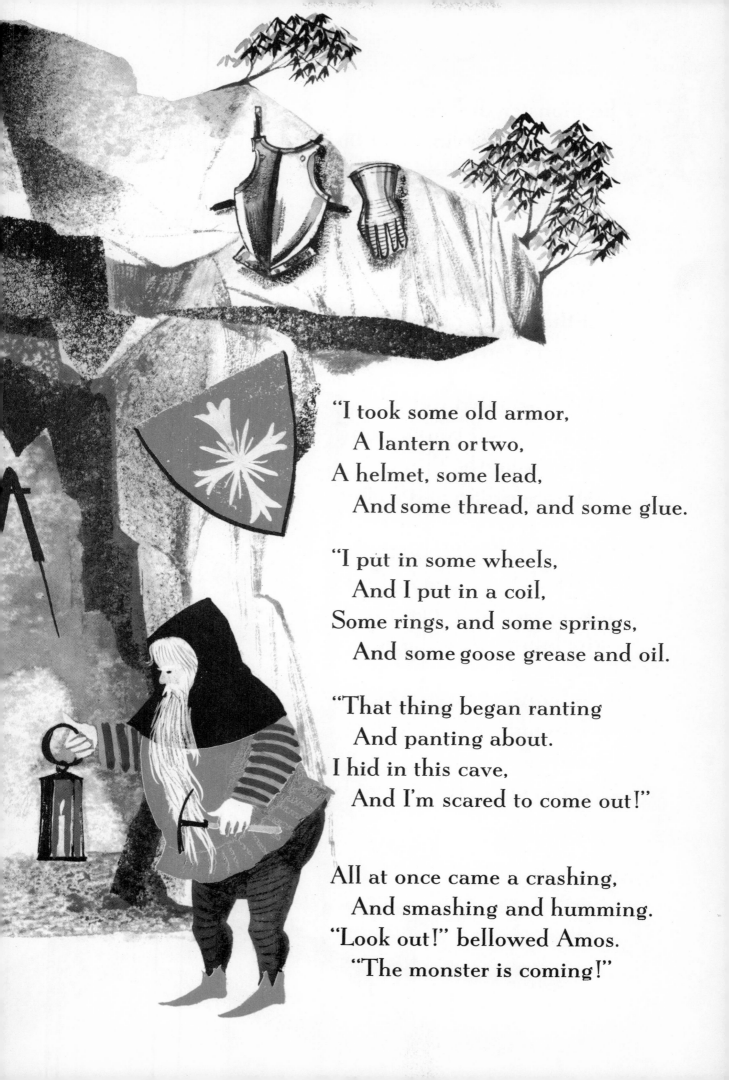

"I took some old armor,
  A lantern or two,
A helmet, some lead,
  And some thread, and some glue.

"I put in some wheels,
  And I put in a coil,
Some rings, and some springs,
  And some goose grease and oil.

"That thing began ranting
  And panting about.
I hid in this cave,
  And I'm scared to come out!"

All at once came a crashing,
  And smashing and humming.
"Look out!" bellowed Amos.
  "The monster is coming!"

The monster *did* come
  But small Kevin stood fast.
He raised up his sword
  As the creature stormed past.

*Wh*ack! went his sword.
  *Wh*oosh! went his mace.
But the monster roared on,
  At a furious pace.

"Halt!" shouted Kevin.
  "I command you to stop!"
But on went the thing
  With a clomp and a clop.

"I can't stab it," thought Kevin.
  "It's as hard as a kettle.
It won't listen to reason;
  Its brains are all metal.

"So I'll just have to chase it
  Through country and town.
Sooner or later,
  It has *got* to run down!"

He chased it for days,
And he chased it for weeks,
Through meadows and forests
And valleys and creeks.

He chased it up mountains
    And then chased it down . . .
He chased it at last
    Into old Devon town,

Straight past the castle
Of Courtly, the king.
Then, all of a sudden,
Something went PING!

With a BOING! and a WHIRRRRRR!
And a few feeble *ticks* . . .
That monster went down
Like ten tons of bricks!

Right up on its head
     Leaped brave little Kevin,
Looking proud as ten peacocks,
     Or maybe, eleven!

People peeked out of,
     And over and under.
Up went a roar
     Like a crashing of thunder.

ut came the king
   In his long royal gown,
With his silvery sword,
   And his jewel-studded crown.

"The monster is dead, Sire,"
   Said Kevin politely.
And oh, he looked fearless,
   And peerless, and knightly!

The king raised his sword,
   And he touched Kevin's head.
"I dub you Sir Kevin of Devon!"
   He said.

ong live Sir Kevin!"
  The townsfolk cried,
"The bravest knight
  in the countryside!"

And there stood Kevin,
  with eyes all bright.
He had dreamed his dream.
  He'd been ready to fight.
He had proved himself worthy
  of being a knight!